# h2o ™
## Just add water!

# First Crush

Read other titles in the series

Just add
water!

# First Crush

Adapted by Sue Behrent

**SIMON AND SCHUSTER**

**SIMON AND SCHUSTER**

First published in Great Britain in 2010 by Simon & Schuster UK Ltd,
1st Floor, 222 Gray's Inn Road, London WC1X 8HB

A CBS Company

Originally published in Australia in 2007 by Parragon
Licenced by ZDF Enterprises GmbH, Mainz

A CIP catalogue record for this book is available from the British Library

ISBN 978-1-84738-773-8

10 9 8 7 6 5 4 3 2 1

Printed by CPI Cox & Wyman, Reading, Berkshire RG1 8EX

# Chapter 1

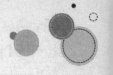

Emma sighed with exasperation as she reached behind her to unhook a rather prickly branch that had caught on her shirt. She almost dropped the box she was carrying as she did so, before almost dropping it again as she tripped on a low-creeping vine. Regaining her composure quickly and blowing a strand of hair out of eyes, she sighed again as she heard Rikki give a squeal of frustration behind her. Emma couldn't see her through the thick foliage that stood between them, but she could have sworn that Rikki had just dropped the box that she was carrying too, and then given it a solid kick for good measure.

It wasn't that Emma resented Lewis for asking them to carry these boxes over to his brother's greenhouse, but did he absolutely have to ask them to do it on a Saturday? And

why *this* Saturday? Lewis knew very well that she had plans to meet up with Byron that day – she must have mentioned it at least twenty times over the past week – and this detour to the greenhouse was definitely going to make her late. *Still*, she thought, as she rested the box on her hip and leaned down to rub her scratched-up ankles, *it* is *Lewis. He's put himself out for us so many times over the last few weeks; I really can't hold this small favour against him.*

*But he could've at least given us some directions*, she thought, stopping again to look around and get her bearings. The greenhouse was huge. And it seemed to have no logical pattern to it at all! Emma felt like they'd been wandering around in circles for ages already and they hadn't caught so much as a glimpse of another human being; just path after path of more and more plants. Every corner they turned, it was more plants! How did Lewis expect them to find him in this maze? She half expected to be rewarded with a prize when they

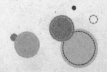

finally reached the centre of it, if there even *was* a centre. Exactly what kind of prize, she couldn't even begin to imagine. Although she did know that Lewis definitely wasn't it. *I hope Byron waits for me*, she thought as she hoisted the box back up and pushed another branch out of her way with her elbow.

"This place is *cool*," Elliot, Emma's little brother, half-whispered a few paces behind her. He'd been like that the whole time they'd been there, going on and on about how amazing the greenhouse was, what an adventure it was! Emma just rolled her eyes at his enthusiasm.

*It's not Jumanji!* she said to herself, half expecting to see an elephant come trumpeting out of the undergrowth. Or a Tyrannosaurus Rex! The place did have the distinct feel of a prehistoric forest…

Emma laughed at herself. *Now who has the overactive imagination?*

Ducking under branches and weaving

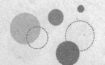
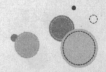

through ferns might've been fun for a kid, but as far as Emma and Rikki were concerned, it was getting old, and it was getting old quickly.

"*Lewis*!!" she shouted through the thick foliage for what felt like the hundredth time. "Where *are* you?"

Finally, as they turned down yet another path that looked just like all the others, something other than a plant suddenly appeared in front of her. Thankfully, it was a friendly face.

Even though she hadn't met him before, Emma guessed it was Lenny, Lewis's brother, straight away. His broad smile reminded her of Lewis in an instant. He might have been older and taller than Lewis, but that smile was unmistakable.

"You're Emma," he said with a big grin when he saw her. "This way." Lenny took the box she was carrying and walked on ahead.

*Finally*, Emma thought with relief, *there's*

*still hope we'll get out of here today.*

"This way, Rikki," she shouted behind her in the general direction she thought Rikki and Elliot must have been. She hoped they weren't too far behind her. *That'd be just my luck*, she thought, *finally finding Lewis and losing those two at the same time.* But she relaxed when she heard their footsteps crunching through the leaves nearby, followed soon after by the sight of Rikki kicking a large and stubborn fern out of the way. Emma gave her what she thought was an encouraging smile as Rikki emerged from between two giant green leaves, trying to reassure her this would all be over soon and they could leave. Rikki poked her tongue out in reply.

"Your friends are here!" Lenny called out to Lewis as they finally arrived at a clearing that Lenny apparently had no trouble finding. It was his greenhouse after all.

"Guys!" Lewis said happily as soon as he saw them, rushing up to Rikki and helping

her lift the heavy box onto a large timber workbench he'd set up in the middle of the clearing. "Great, you got the stuff!"

"Yes, I hope you're going to pay us for all of this, Lewis," said Rikki, getting straight down to business and stretching out her aching arms and back as she spoke.

"Only with my firm friendship," Lewis said with a cheeky smile.

Lenny had already pulled the packing tape off the box Emma had brought in and was rummaging around inside. He hauled out a couple of pipes and hoses and examined them carefully.

"Is this going to work, Lewis?" he asked, sceptically eyeing both the equipment and Lewis in equal measure.

Emma had to admit, as keen as she was to get out of there and go and do her own thing, she was still kind of interested to see what exactly it was that they'd dragged all that way.

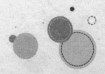

The only instructions Lewis had given them that morning were to pick up some boxes from a hardware store in the shopping centre near Emma's house and meet him at the greenhouse. Picking up the boxes had been no problem at all, but they'd been packed up and ready at the counter of the shop when Rikki and Emma had arrived to collect them, so they hadn't a clue what they contained. Plus they were completely unmarked – just big, plain, brown, *heavy* boxes – and therefore a bit of a mystery.

She and Rikki were intrigued. In fact, while they'd been stumbling around lost in the greenhouse, they'd put bets on what they thought the boxes held.

Rikki thought they were the seeds of a type of exotic plant species, but Emma was sure it would be something much more mundane and Lewis-like; her bet was that it was science equipment of some description.

All Emma could see as she watched Lewis

unpack the boxes was reel after reel of black rubber hose, not the flasks and beakers she'd been expecting and definitely not Rikki's seeds. It turned out they were both wrong! *Still*, she thought, satisfied, *whatever the hoses are for, at least my guess was closer to the mark than Rikki's.* But why was Lenny asking if it was going to work? Would *what* work?

"Sure it is, Lenny, of *course*," Lewis answered confidently as he sorted the hoses and some clamps into neat piles on the bench.

"Oh, *this* is Lenny?" Emma interrupted. Obviously she already knew exactly who Lenny was, but she couldn't let Lewis get away with not introducing them properly.

*He really does have the worst manners*, she thought to herself, *although Cleo doesn't seem to mind. Perhaps she likes the scatter-brained professor type!*

"Oh, what? You haven't met?" Lewis said absently, his head buried in one of the boxes.

"Lenny, the guys; the guys, Lenny, my brother, second oldest."

"How many brothers have you got?" asked Rikki, craning her neck to see if there was actually anything *interesting* in the box. She was just as keen as Emma to find out what they'd carted all this way.

"Four," Lewis answered as he upended the last box and emptied out a few stray bolts and brackets, "but only one who would own a plant nursery."

"And only one who would hire Lewis to fix a watering system," Lenny added with a grin.

*Right*, thought Emma. *Of course! A watering system – nursery, watering system – that makes sense.*

"Hey, you're getting a good deal here, Lenny," Lewis said, waving a screwdriver around absently as he spoke. "The whole cross-sector irrigation system will be completely automated, and far superior to that ancient

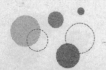

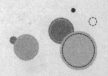

sprinkler system up there."

Suddenly, Emma and Rikki weren't interested in what Lewis was doing with hoses and tubes. The moment he'd mentioned sprinklers 'up there', their gaze had become fixed on the network of pipes and nozzles that hung threateningly above their heads, each nozzle looking like an outdoor shower waiting to happen – waiting to turn both of them into mermaids in an instant – not exactly the kind of show they wanted to put on in front of Elliot and Lenny.

As if they didn't already have enough reasons not to stick around – boredom being one of them, suddenly they had a much bigger one.

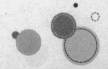

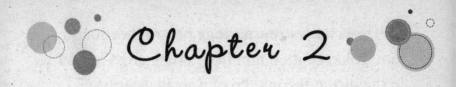

# Chapter 2

"Okay," said Emma immediately, already backing her way out of the clearing. "Well, it seems like you two have got a lot to talk about, so we'll be heading off." She only hoped getting *out* of there would be a lot quicker than getting *in*.

The only thing left to do was to find Elliot. Emma was sure he had been with Rikki when they'd arrived in the clearing, but now that she thought about it, she couldn't remember seeing him there. She guessed he must have got fed up and wandered off to explore the greenhouse some more while they'd been watching Lewis unpack the boxes. With any luck, he hadn't wandered too far away.

"Elliot, where are you?" Rikki called out as they hurried back along the paths. *He can't have got far*, she thought.

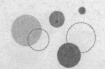 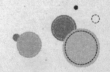

Thankfully, it wasn't long before they found him. Rikki spotted him first, sitting cross-legged in the dirt in the middle of a small clearing between some ferns, with a strange, awe-struck look on his face.

"You could hide here *forever*," said Elliot mysteriously when he saw her.

*Whatever, you little weirdo!* thought Rikki. She didn't have a lot of experience with kids and he was kind of freaking her out! What was he doing hiding in the bushes anyway?

"Maybe you should," Rikki suggested jokingly, wondering what the world would be like with fewer of her friends' little brothers hanging around.

"Come on, Elliot," Emma said before he had a chance to answer back. She squeezed past Rikki and grabbed Elliot's arm, hauling him up to his feet and almost dragging him back onto the path. "We've got to get you to surfing practice."

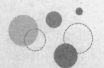
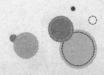

"Whoa, wait a minute! Did you say *surfing*?" asked Rikki, still rooted to the spot. She was sure Emma hadn't mentioned anything about surfing practice when they'd arranged to meet up that morning. As far as she was concerned, she and Emma were heading straight to the beach to meet up with Byron. At least, that had been the original plan before the whole box-carrying-greenhouse thing had been thrown into the mix. But there'd definitely been no plans involving a little brother and she was absolutely certain there'd been no mention of surfing practice.

"Yeah, Byron's teaching him," Emma said, as if there was nothing wrong at all. "He's doing really well."

"Mmm, that's *great*," Rikki said sarcastically, "but aren't you forgetting something?" Surely Emma couldn't have forgotten what happened when they got wet. No. The idea was ridiculous. After all, Emma's the sensible one, Rikki thought to herself. She or Cleo may have been

a bit careless from time to time, but not Emma. But then, why would Emma suddenly think that taking her brother to surfing practice was a good idea? There had to be a catch.

"Relax," Emma replied simply as she turned back onto the path and started walking briskly towards the greenhouse gate. "I'm not going near the water. And neither is he!" she shouted back over her shoulder.

Rikki stood and looked sceptically at her friend's retreating back.

*I could say something about this not being part of the plan or I could give Emma the benefit of the doubt and avoid the stupid arguments I usually get into!* she thought, absentmindedly kicking an oddly speckled rock onto the path in front of her. *Not every difference of opinion needs to turn into a major deal!*

Rikki had actually been quite pleased when Emma had asked her to the beach, although she hadn't said as much. Usually it would have

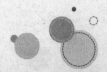

been Cleo who got invited, but since Cleo had started her job at the marine park and didn't have quite so much spare time available, Emma had asked Rikki to hang out a few times and she was glad they were getting to do more things together.

Rikki could tell that Emma was nervous about meeting up with Byron too, and not just because she'd mentioned it a hundred times that week, but because she obviously wanted a friend along as support. *A friend…* Rikki smiled to herself. It wasn't that long ago when she'd thought Emma was uptight and prissy and goodness knows what Emma had thought of her! Although Rikki had a pretty good idea.

It would've been nice to get a heads up about all the other plans though. *Still*, she thought as she hurried to catch up with them, *perhaps it might be a good afternoon, even with Elliot tagging along.*

The whole way to the beach, Elliot talked non-stop about his surfing lesson and what a fantastic teacher Byron was. Inside, Emma felt pleased. Not only because Elliot was having such an excellent time but because it also gave her an excellent excuse to spend more time with Byron.

*He might be a surf god, but he's a really nice guy too!* thought Emma, feeling happy about how the day was turning out.

Rikki, on the other hand, was not feeling happy at all! Elliot's constant chat was driving her around the bend!

Rikki had to admit though, as soon as she stepped off the scratchy grass and onto the beach properly, her feet sank into the warm crunchy softness of the sand and everything started to seem better. It was just a pity they wouldn't have a chance to go for a swim. It was frustrating; being *so* close to the water and not being able to sprint up to the shore-break

and dive straight in like she usually did. *No mermaid action for me today*, she thought with a touch of regret.

Still, there were worse things than having the whole afternoon to spend on the beach on such a beautiful day. And if she had to stretch out on a towel and soak up the rays, then Rikki figured she might *just* be able to cope with a few small inconveniences.

Elliot's voice cut sharply through Rikki's thoughts.

"… and when I wiped out that time, I had sand all through my wetsuit and Mum said she wasn't going to let me have any more lessons if I tracked sand all through the house again, didn't she Em?" he said.

*Sand? Huh?* thought Rikki, as she looked questioningly at Emma.

"The first few lessons are on the sand… *well away* from the water," Emma said as they

walked swiftly along the beach. "No chance of getting wet," she added meaningfully.

"*Ahhhh*, so we get to lie there listening to Byron shouting instructions at Elliot?" Rikki asked a little sarcastically, as if she could think of much more relaxing ways to work on her tan.

"*Something* like that," Emma replied, rolling her eyes at Rikki's tone. Not even Rikki's teasing could stop her from having a good day. All she had to do now was find Byron and her day would be just about perfect.

Elliot had charged off ahead of them and was the first to spot Byron in the distance, standing by a rocky outcrop where the beach started to curve around to the point. He was talking to a group of about six or seven younger surfers, all of them hanging on his every word.

"There's Byron, Em!" exclaimed Elliot as he took off down the beach to join the group.

Emma breathed a quiet sigh of relief; she was glad that Byron had waited for them. But

now she felt another emotion wash over her…
anxiety.

*I'm pathetic!* she thought, disappointed with
herself for being nervous. But the closer she
and Rikki got to Byron, the worse she felt!

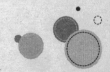

# Chapter 3

"*Revolting*!" said Byron disgustedly as he picked up a grotty plastic bag from the sand as Emma and Rikki approached.

"Hey, Emma!" he called out in greeting. "The Clean Up the Beach Rally is starting soon. Are you still coming?"

Emma gulped.

"Oh, I'd forgotten about that," she replied, trying to keep the embarrassment from her voice. *How could I have forgotten about the rally?* she thought to herself angrily. With everything that had happened that morning and the rush to get to the beach, it had completely slipped her mind. All week she'd been thinking about meeting up with Byron and she'd ended up forgetting the *real* reason they were meeting up in the first place. Elliot's surfing lessons had been going on for about three weeks

now – their parents had organized it – but last week when she dropped Elliot at the beach, she and Byron had ended up chatting for a while. They'd got on to the subject of how dirty the beach was and how people didn't respect the environment and Byron had told her how angry it made him. "People come down to the beach to swim and sunbathe and to have a good time, but they don't care about the state they leave it in! All their rubbish gets washed away by the tide and they think that's okay! But if they knew what happened to their junk... how sea mammals get captured in their plastic bags and... it just makes me *so* mad!" he'd spluttered. It was then that Byron had asked Emma if she wanted to go to the Clean Up the Beach Rally with him.

Now here was Emma having to admit she'd forgotten about it!

"Wait a sec," she said, suddenly thinking of a way *they* could still go to the Rally and *Elliot* could still get his surfing practice.

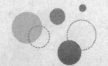

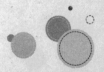

Emma looked at Rikki pleadingly.

"Can you do me a *really* big favour?" she asked.

Rikki had a feeling she knew what was coming next and she wasn't thrilled about it!

"Could you watch Elliot for me *please*?" Emma finished.

"*No*," Rikki replied without any hesitation at all. She was *not* going to spend the afternoon with some kid while her friend went off to save the world. Rikki couldn't believe that Emma was even asking her! "No *way*," she added firmly, shaking her head in case Emma didn't get it. "It's *not* going to happen."

"*Please*?!" asked Emma again, feeling like her one and only chance with Byron was slipping away.

"Sorry, I don't do kids," replied Rikki, not seeing what the problem was. "Just take him with you."

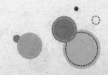

Elliot and Byron, meanwhile, had wandered off to where Byron's surfboard lay on the sand and were running through a few manoeuvres that Elliot had already learned in previous lessons.

Even from that distance Byron could see that something was up and caught the very end of Rikki's and Emma's conversation.

"He can't come with us; he needs to practise," he called out, gesturing to Elliot. Both girls glanced down at Elliot who lay sprawled face down in the sand.

*He really needs to work on his technique!* Rikki snickered to herself as Elliot got up and spat out the sand he'd managed to get in his mouth.

Emma realized she'd need to try another tactic if she was ever going to persuade Rikki to stay there with Elliot.

"Maybe *you* want to come to the Clean Up the Beach Rally?" she suggested, knowing how

much Rikki would *hate* the idea.

Rikki screwed up her face.

"No thanks," she replied, just as Emma knew she would.

"Okay-great-settled-thanks-appreciate it!" garbled Emma as she hastily collected up her things. "Come on, Byron," she shouted, moving off towards him, "let's get going; we don't want to miss the Rally!"

Rikki frowned, knowing she didn't have a choice in the matter. If she said something now, she'd look like a terrible person who was trying to ruin her friend's chances with a boy!

With her shoulders set in resignation, Rikki watched on as Emma and Byron trudged their way up the beach, their heads bent together happily in conversation.

*I've totally been taken advantage of!* she thought to herself heatedly. "I take no responsibility for anything that may or may not happen to him!" she shouted at Emma and

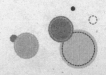

Byron's backs as they continued walking away.

Emma turned around, shading her eyes from the sun.

"I trust you!" she yelled back, giving Rikki a friendly wave.

Rikki kicked the sand in frustration.

*Fantastic!* Rikki thought sarcastically. *Just great! Apparently this is how I spend my Saturday afternoons now, looking after little brothers!! Not only can't I go for a swim, but now I can't even just lie here enjoying the sun. No, I have to be Ms Responsible, while she goes off with Mr I'm-a-big-shot-surfer to save the environment!!! Really, how did I end up in this mess?*

"Did you know I'm gonna be a pro surfer?" said Elliot, suddenly appearing at her side.

Rikki glared down at him.

*Fabulous*, thought Rikki, *now I'm stuck with Mr-wanna-be-big-shot surfer.* "No-one said I

have to talk to you," she snapped back at him irritably.

"Watch, I'll show you!" Elliot said, ignoring her tone. Grinning broadly he raced over and collected the surfboard from where it lay against the rocks before dashing off towards the shoreline.

Within seconds he'd reached the water and begun to wade through the shallows.

"Elliot! Quit showing off!" Rikki called after him, walking as far as she dared towards the water. As if she didn't have enough to deal with, now the kid was getting an ego!

But Elliot took no notice of her.

"Elliot! Come back here," she shouted again, becoming increasingly alarmed the further Elliot went. But Elliot just settled himself flat on the surfboard and paddled out through the shore-break. "I mean it, Elliot!" she yelled in her most adult voice, "I'll leave you here!"

But it was too late! Rikki saw the first

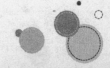

serious wave build up long before Elliot did and even from the beach she saw the look of surprise and fear on his face as the wave pitched up in front of him and crashed down on his head, knocking him right off the board. And before either of them really knew what had happened, Elliot, coughing and spluttering, disappeared under the waves.

Brat or not, when Elliot's head popped up to the surface, Rikki felt sick with relief!

But even though he was out of immediate danger, Elliot was obviously still in a lot of trouble. His board had been swept away by the current and was far out of his reach. And it looked to Rikki as if he was only just managing to keep his head above water.

Rikki knew she had to act fast!

She quickly looked up and down the beach to see if anyone was around. There were a few people around in the distance; a dad playing beach-cricket with his kids and a couple

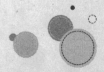

walking hand-in-hand in the opposite direction, but for the moment, no one was paying any attention to either her or Elliot.

"Help!" Elliot shouted desperately, his voice muffled by waves crashing about him. "Someone help!"

Even above the thundering din of the waves, Rikki could hear the panic in Elliot's voice. He was in real trouble. Without thinking of the consequences, she sprinted the rest of the way down to the shore and dove straight into the shallow water. Within seconds she felt the power of her mermaid's tail whip through the ocean and send her speeding towards Elliot.

*Wait*, she thought, stopping suddenly with a swift flick of her tail. *I can't let him see me like this! What am I thinking?* She hadn't had time to think; that was the problem. *If only I could get to him without him seeing anything, I might be able to save him and myself. But how?*

Suddenly, she remembered the surfboard.

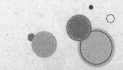

*Of course!* she thought, *if I can hide behind the board and keep it in front of me the whole time, Elliot won't see a thing.*

Then, with another powerful flick of her tail, she spun around in the water and sped towards the drifting surfboard, hurriedly grabbing it before flipping back around beneath the water and darting swiftly back towards Elliot. She covered the distance between them with just two flicks of her tail, reaching him just in time to shove the board under his stomach as he began to sink beneath the surface again.

Elliot clutched the surfboard tightly and gasped desperately for air, the miserable look of fear on his face gradually disappearing as he began to regain his composure, only to be replaced by a look of curiosity.

"How did you do that?" he spluttered out between more gulps of air.

"Get on and shut up!" Rikki told him sharply. She didn't have time for any questions.

Every second that ticked by only increased Elliot's chances of seeing her scales, or worse, her tail.

She had to get Elliot to the shore before he recovered sufficiently enough to ask her any more impossible-to-answer questions!

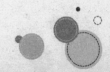

# Chapter 4

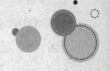

"Next time, wear your leg-rope," she added, before whipping her tail through the water once more with a single, powerful swish that propelled Elliot and the board swiftly and safely back to the beach.

Or at least, that's what Rikki had intended to do. What she didn't realize as she let go of the board was that that last flick of her tail had been so forceful that not only did it send Elliot bouncing across the water to the shore, but it sent him half way up the beach as well!

Elliot landed with a violent jolt, which sent him flying off the surfboard, landing headfirst in the sand.

Eventually, Elliot sat up and looked around. To the right of him lay the surfboard. He breathed a sigh of relief; he didn't know *how*

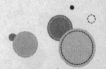

he would've explained losing the surfboard to Byron!

Still dazed and taking a while to get his bearings, he suddenly noticed three grooves etched deeply into the sand, trailing back from the the fins of the board right down to the water's edge. Elliot shook his head in amazement and wondered how it was possible that his fins could have left such severe marks! He couldn't quite remember exactly what had happened, but he *definitely* knew that Rikki had swum at an incredible speed to reach him in time to get his board safely under him. *But how did I get back to the beach? Did I paddle that fast?* he wondered to himself, as he stared at the marks in the sand.

While Elliot was still sitting there coming to grips with what had just happened, the softness of the sand muffled the footsteps of Zane and Nate from behind him so that Elliot didn't even hear them approach.

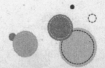

"Hey Elliot, what's this?" asked Zane, pointing to the gouges the fins had left.

Elliot jumped in fright at the sound of Zane's voice, but ignored the question. He was far too caught up in figuring out how he'd got back to the beach.

"How'd you *do* that?" Nate asked, his voice full of admiration of the power it must have taken to ride a surfboard up onto the beach like that.

But Elliot wasn't listening at all. All his attention was focused out to sea as he searched for any sign of Rikki.

Nate and Zane looked at each other and snickered, eventually walking away when Elliot still hadn't responded. Even ten minutes later when Zane and Nate were walking back the way they'd come, Elliot still sat on the beach in exactly the same position, his eyes still scanning the horizon.

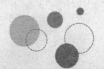

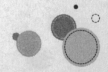

At home that night, Emma was thinking about the Clean Up the Beach Rally. Hanging out with Byron had been cool. They'd walked to the rally together and talked about how he'd got into surfing and how much she still loved swimming, even though she'd given it up competitively. It had been really nice being around him and she felt they were starting to get to know each other. It was amazing how much they had in common. But the rally itself hadn't been *anything* like what she'd thought it would be.

She'd thought the people there would be more motivated to actually *do* something about cleaning up the beach. But instead, it was all talk. And what made things worse was that at the end of it all, as people started to leave, she was horrified to see that the park where the rally had been held was filthier than it had been before they arrived!

But going along to the rally wasn't the *only* thing Emma regretted. Ever since she'd got

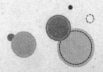

home, all she'd heard was Elliot's voice going on and on about how absolutely *awesome* Rikki was.

At first she'd barely listened, but as Elliot talked relentlessly on, she'd tuned in and had begun to realize what must've happened after she'd gone off with Byron. As the story unfolded, she wished she'd never left him with Rikki!

*Is this the price I have to pay for hanging out with Byron*, she thought as she sat listening to Elliot's enthusiastic explanation. *Because right now, the price seems* way *too high.*

And when their parents arrived home, Elliot began all over again! How *amazing* Rikki was. How *incredible* Rikki was. It seemed to Elliot's family that he'd never shut up about Super-Rikki!

"It was like this rip came out of nowhere," said Elliot, almost bouncing around the kitchen with excitement while his mum got dinner ready. "I thought I was going to end up in New

Zealand or somewhere! And then, she was *there*... she saved me."

"Wait a second," Emma interrupted him, suddenly looking up from the history assignment she was working on at the kitchen table. "You *saw* Rikki... in the water?" Suddenly Emma wished she'd paid more attention to what Elliot had said earlier.

"Yeah, she was unbelievable!" Elliot said, stealing one of the chips his mum had just taken out of the oven.

"Really?" Emma asked casually, not wanting to let Elliot or her parents know she had any reason to be suspicious. "Why?"

"Cos she's the fastest swimmer I've *ever* seen," Elliot replied. "She could beat anything, even a dolphin!"

"A dolphin?" Emma asked, still trying to sound casual but feeling more anxious by the second. "Elliot, what *exactly* did you see out there?"

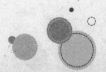

36

*And what didn't you see?* she added to herself. *How could Rikki be so careless!*

"What *I* want to know, Elliot," their dad interrupted, looking up from his newspaper with a very stern expression, "is what were you doing in the water in the first place?"

"Oh, well ... I ..." Elliot stumbled for an excuse.

Luckily for him, the doorbell suddenly chimed.

"I'll get it," said Elliot, exiting the kitchen as quickly as he could and avoiding his father's question.

He raced to the front door and flung it open.

"*Rikki!*" yelled Elliot excitedly, when he saw who it was. He still had *so* many questions to ask her about what had happened at the beach, he hardly knew where to start!

"Where did you go?" he began, leaving Rikki to stand on the doorstep. "You saved

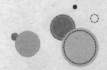

me, but then you disappeared. How did you do that?"

"I'm… good at holding my breath," was all Rikki could think to say, shrugging as if it was nothing.

"*Good*? Are you kidding? You were *awesome*," said Elliot, gazing up at her in awe. "No, wait, you're *amazing*. Wait, you're *incredible*!"

*I can't take much more of this!* thought Rikki uncomfortably, *I only pulled the little brat out of the water.*

"Do me a favour will you?" she asked impatiently.

"*Anything*," Elliot answered, sounding like he genuinely *would* do absolutely anything for her.

"Let me in?" Rikki suggested with raised eyebrows.

"You got it!" he replied eagerly, holding the

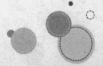

door wide open for her. "Rikki's here!"

Rikki stuck her finger in her ear and wiggled it around. She suspected she might've lost some hearing in her right ear, given her proximity to Elliot's bellowing!

In the kitchen, the rest of the family exchanged glances. They knew what Elliot was like when he was enthusiastic about something. Emma hoped Rikki could cope!

"Come on in, hero," Emma's dad said as soon as Rikki came into the kitchen, putting his paper down and getting up from the table to greet her.

"We owe you a debt of gratitude," her mum added, suddenly throwing her arms around Rikki without warning. In her eagerness, Emma's mum hadn't even bothered to take her oven-mitts off and Rikki could feel the heat from the baking tray she'd been holding through her shirt.

"I was just telling them how you saved me,"

39

Elliot said proudly.

"Oh, oh I wouldn't call it *saving* exactly," Rikki mumbled, her voice slightly muffled under Emma's mum's hug. *This is so embarrassing*, she thought. *All I did was give him a bit of a push back to the beach. Anyone else would have done exactly the same thing.*

"Hah, modest as well as brave," Emma's mum went on, hugging Rikki even tighter.

"She's the fastest swimmer in the world!" said Elliot, dancing around the two women with delight.

"He's exaggerating," Rikki said in her defence, disengaging herself from Emma's mum's bear hug and backing hastily away to the other side of the kitchen table.

"Nonsense!" Emma's dad objected. "What you did was nothing short of magnificent."

All of a sudden Rikki could see *exactly* where Elliot got his high levels of keenness from!

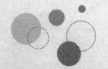
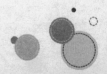

"Rikki?" Emma finally interrupted. "Can I talk to you for a second… in private?" It was just the kind of escape route Rikki had been looking for. *Finally*, she thought to herself as she gave Emma's parents an apologetic smile and followed Emma out of the kitchen and up the stairs to her room, *I knew Emma would get me out of this. At least she'll understand what really happened out there.*

As she followed Emma up the stairs, Rikki was looking forward to finding out how things had gone with Byron and the rally.

But by the time they got up to her room, the look on Emma's face as she expectantly held the door open for her told Rikki she wasn't being rescued at all, and she wasn't about to find out anything about Byron. Emma was angry. In fact, if the tight line of her mouth was anything to go by, she was furious.

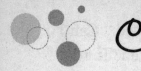

# Chapter 5

"What?" Rikki asked defensively as soon as Emma closed her bedroom door. She couldn't believe that Emma could be angry with her. After all, she'd just saved her brother – anyone would think she might actually be a bit happy about that!

"You take a swim, and you ask me *'what'*?" Emma snapped back. She *was* furious.

"You left me to baby-sit," Rikki defended herself. This was not the kind of rescue she'd hoped for at all. "I did the job. Next time let someone else clean up the world while you look after him yourself."

"Don't worry, I will," Emma said coldly, although her voice did sound *slightly* calmer. Rikki *had* just saved her little brother, but she'd taken such a massive risk... Elliot could've seen

42

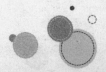

Rikki's tail and realized that the diary that Cleo had been writing about them being mermaids hadn't been a fictional English assignment after all – it'd been fact!

"Did he, you know, *see* anything?" Emma asked, more gently.

Finally, Rikki realized what Emma was so angry about. *So that's it*, she thought. *She thinks I let him see that I'm a mermaid! What kind of an idiot does she think I am? I saved her brother; shouldn't that be all that matters right now? And she should know that I'd never do anything to put our secret at risk. Why can't she just be happy and leave it at that?*

"Rikki, did he see anything?" Emma asked again, more insistently.

"Other than when I flashed him you mean?" Rikki answered finally. Emma paled slightly in horror, her lips pressed tightly together.

For a second, Rikki *wanted* her to be outraged. But then she quickly realized she'd

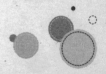

had enough drama for one day. All she wanted now was to hang out with her friend and talk about the things they usually talked about.

"Lighten up," Rikki said eventually, throwing herself onto Emma's bed. "He doesn't suspect a thing."

"Well, why is he out there raving about how you could out-swim a dolphin?" Emma asked stubbornly, pacing around the room.

"He's exaggerating," Rikki answered as patiently as she could. "I was careful. I made sure he didn't see anything. I'm not *stupid*, Emma, so stop treating me like I am!"

"I didn't mean that," Emma said apologetically as she sat down on her bed next to Rikki and folded her legs beneath her, "it's just that finding out we're mermaids would be huge for Elliot."

"Duh, yeah," said Rikki, rolling her eyes. "I'm pretty sure it'd be huge for *anyone*."

"You don't understand," Emma explained.

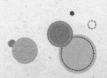

"We've *never* had secrets. This'd be like one massive lie to him. He'd never be able to handle it."

Emma recalled one year when the family had thrown Elliot a surprise birthday party. Three weeks before, they'd sent out the invitations to Elliot's friends and on the day of the party their dad had taken Elliot down to the shopping centre to check out a sports store while the guests arrived and took their places.

But when they'd got home and Elliot's friends had jumped out from their hiding places and yelled SURPRISE, Elliot had burst into tears and run upstairs to his room. It took a lot of coaxing to get him to come back down to the party and even more effort to get Elliot to tell them *why* he'd been so upset. "Everyone knew about it except *me*!" Elliot had snivelled. "You were all talking behind my back about this great thing you were organizing and you didn't include me!" It had taken a few years after that before anyone in Emma's family would even

*mention* the words 'surprise party'!

Emma knew how devastated Elliot would be if he stumbled upon their secret mermaid business. It would be a million times worse than the surprise birthday party.

"He'd never be able to *handle* it? Funny that," Rikki said bitterly, folding her arms as she spoke. "People who grow up in perfect families seem to have that problem – they can't handle anything."

Rikki didn't want to be nasty, she really didn't, but she'd had enough. Why should she have to console Emma like this? In the end Elliot hadn't *seen* anything, didn't *know* anything and as far as Rikki could see he'd had quite a good time with her, all things considered! He was certainly having an awesome time telling and retelling the story! If Emma was feeling guilty about keeping secrets from her brother then that was *her* problem, not Rikki's.

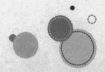

The creak of the door caught both girls' attention and they hastily jumped to their feet. Cleo's nose, followed by the rest of her head, poked through the gap between the door and doorframe. Rikki and Emma both sighed with relief; Emma's parents must've let Cleo in while they'd been arguing.

Cleo, of course, already knew the entire story. Elliot had opened the door to her downstairs and on seeing who it was, had immediately launched into what a super-star Rikki was and how she'd saved his life.

So when Cleo came into Emma's room and had closed the door behind her, she hadn't even sat down before she launched straight into the same line of attack on Rikki that Emma had only just finished!

"I understand you took a calculated risk, Rikki," Cleo lectured. "But... *wow*. We can't risk turning into mermaids on a public beach."

Rikki bit her lip determinedly and mustered

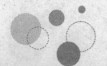
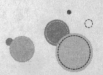

all of her willpower to stop herself from raising her voice. She could almost understand Emma accusing her of being careless, but from Cleo it was just *too* much. It was as if the whole pool thing at Miriam's party had never happened; as if she hadn't chosen to get a job at the marine park of all places. Why couldn't her friends just trust her?

"Elliot's home safe, there's no drama," Rikki said finally, trying desperately to keep her voice calm and to convince them both that they were totally overreacting. "Can we *please* drop this?" she said insistently.

Cleo and Emma looked at each other. Perhaps they had lectured Rikki enough for one evening.

"Just be careful next time," Emma told her.

*There'll never* be a 'next time', Rikki thought to herself. *I'm never going to mind another kid brother again after all this hassle!*

Aloud, Rikki sighed theatrically. "I'm *always*

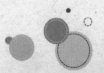

careful, Mum," she said sarcastically, leaning back on Emma's desk as she spoke and sending a full glass of water spilling all over Emma's homework. The water drenched everything, running haphazardly over the desk before dripping down onto the carpet in a steady, soaking, stream.

"My geography assignment!" Emma shrieked, jumping up from the bed to stare helplessly at the mess. "Rikki, I was almost finished. It took me hours!"

"Uh, we only got that assignment *yesterday*, and you're almost done?" Rikki said, completely ignoring how upset Emma was.

"She *was* almost done," Cleo corrected her.

"Thanks to you, I'll have to start from scratch," Emma said, clearly upset by the thought.

Rikki felt a bit guilty, but what could she do about it now? The homework was ruined and no apology was going to bring it back!

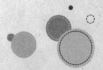

She grabbed a couple of tissues from a box on the shelf above Emma's desk and mopped up the water as best as she could from the carpet. But just as Rikki was about to try and blot the water off the actual assignment, Emma jumped off the bed and pushed her hand away.

"No, don't, you'll *blur* it!" she shouted.

Rikki stepped back. She kind of felt like laughing, it was just too absurd how uptight Emma was!

*Oh, my powers will be able to sort this out in a sec!* thought Rikki suddenly. She didn't know why she hadn't thought of that sooner!

"Okay, wait," Rikki said, stifling her snickers. She dropped the tissues into the bin and raised her hand steadily over the sodden assignment, focusing all of her concentration on the paper. Gently and slowly, she began to heat it from within, gradually increasing the temperature towards boiling point. Slowly, steam began to rise as the water evaporated out.

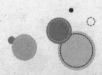

The paper started to dry. *Phew!* Rikki thought, *at least that's one disaster averted for the day.*

"*See…?* no need to stress," she said confidently. But just as quickly as her spirits rose, they plummeted again as the paper abruptly overheated and turned into a dry, shrivelled, black lump before her eyes.

Rikki stared at the ashy mess and exhaled loudly.

"Oops," was all she could think to say.

"*Oops?*" Emma spat, clearly unimpressed.

"It was an accident," Rikki said, throwing up her hands in frustration. She'd been annoyed with herself in the first place for knocking over the water and now she was even more annoyed that her powers hadn't been able to make everything okay again.

"*Wait!* Maybe I can reverse it," Cleo suggested, "put some water molecules back in!" Then without hesitation, she reached out her hand towards the desk and focused her

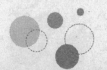
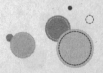

mind on the paper, feeling for whatever water molecules remained and manipulating them to her will. For a moment, with her eyes closed in concentration, she felt the molecules fall into place, multiplying and re-hydrating the paper, but when she opened her eyes and looked at her handiwork, the paper had simply turned into a gooey, clumpy pulp that all the powers in the world wouldn't be able to fix!

Both Emma and Rikki raised their eyebrows at Cleo.

"Um... *oops*?" Cleo offered sheepishly.

"*Cleo*!" Emma said, even more annoyed than before.

"We're *all* still learning how to use our powers, Em," Cleo told her reassuringly, putting her arm around her as she said it.

"And we've all got to get better... *fast*," Emma said seriously, looking both Rikki and Cleo directly in the eye as she got to her feet, and saying what all three of them already knew.

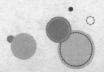

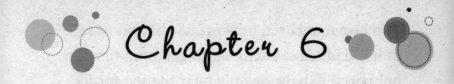

# Chapter 6

Thankfully, Emma quickly forgot all about having to re-do her geography homework once they got talking about the rally and hanging out with Byron!

Rikki hadn't been surprised to hear what the rally had been like, but Cleo was noticeably disappointed.

"What did you expect?" Rikki asked, when Emma told them about the rubbish that was left at the park after everyone had gone. "You thought they'd be different from everyone else just because they went to a rally?"

"Rikki! Don't be so cynical," Cleo said. "There are people out there who really do want to make a difference. What about my dad? He did something when he found out what was happening to the sea turtles." Cleo smiled

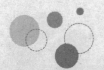

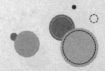

as she remembered how proud she had been of her dad for standing up to Johnno when he'd been fishing illegally near the sea turtles' nesting beaches.

"Yeah, well maybe there *are* some people who actually care," Rikki admitted. "But I wouldn't bet there were very many."

"Anyway," Rikki went on, eager to change the subject. "Enough about the rally – tell us more about what happened with Byron."

But before Emma could go into any more detail on that score, they were interrupted by a timid knock at Emma's bedroom door.

"Come in," Emma called out, as the door slowly swung open to reveal a very nervous-looking Elliot standing in the doorway. He clutched something behind his back and shuffled uncertainly from one foot to the other as though he wasn't quite sure whether he wanted to come in or not.

"Hi," Elliot said hesitantly as he gazed

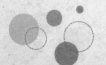
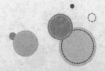

straight past Emma and Cleo to where Rikki still stood beside Emma's desk. "Rikki, this is for you," he said, stepping gingerly around the bed and holding out a small envelope to her.

"Uh," Rikki stammered, reluctantly taking the envelope. She didn't want to open it, but Elliot just stood there, looking up at her expectantly as if he wasn't going to make a move until she did. Rikki looked up quickly to Emma and Cleo, glaring at them in the hope that they'd do something to make Elliot leave, but they both just shrugged their shoulders as if to say she was on her own.

Seeing that she had no other option, Rikki reluctantly tore open the envelope, pulled out a card and started to read. "Dear Rikki", she read silently to herself, "You are my hero. Love Elliot."

Rikki felt a little queasy in the pit of her stomach and didn't know where to look. And she certainly didn't have a clue what she should *say* to Elliot!

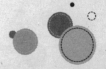

Emma could see how embarrassed Rikki was and how she obviously had no idea how to react!

"Elliot, that's *so* nice," Emma said, smiling sweetly. "Isn't it *nice*, Rikki?"

Rikki silently thanked Emma for jumping in when she did; otherwise things could've turned extremely awkward. *Extremely.*

"Uh, yeah, that's… that's great," Rikki agreed, trying really hard to sound convincing. "Thanks."

Cleo and Emma breathed a sigh of relief. So what if they noticed the insincerity in Rikki's voice, as long as Elliot didn't!

And he clearly hadn't heard a hint of dishonesty in Rikki's reply, because he quickly said. "Do you wanna come play my new 3D skate game?"

"She'd *love* to," Emma answered for her.

"Except, that…" Rikki jumped in, frowning

at Emma to keep her mouth shut. "Except I...
have... to..." she racked her brains frantically
for an even half-decent excuse not to be able to
play. *Any* excuse would do.

"Except that I have to be somewhere
right about now actually," Rikki blurted out,
completely aware of how lame an excuse it was,
but not really caring.

"Sorry," she said to Elliot as she edged past
him towards the door. " See ya."

Rikki gave a little wave that took in the
entire room and was just about to shut the door
behind her when she heard Elliot call out.

"Wait," he said. "I got you these as well.
They're chocolates."

From behind his back, Elliot produced a
box of chocolates wrapped with obvious care
in garish pink spangly paper and tied up with a
hideous looking purple-flecked bow.

"Oh, *chocolates*, yum," said Rikki as she
accepted the gift and held it at arms length like

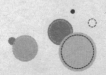

it was a box of snakes. "*Thanks*."

"They're the best ones I could find," Elliot told her enthusiastically. "I used *all* my savings. And I hope you like the soft centres. If you don't I can take them back."

"No, no. Soft centres are fine. Thanks," Rikki mumbled, trying desperately to think of a way to get out of such an incredibly embarrassing situation. She looked daggers at Emma and Cleo. *Do something about this!*

"Elliot," Emma said, gently interrupting, "Can I talk to you for a minute?"

"Sure," Elliot answered happily, before turning to Rikki. "Don't go away," he told her with a wink as he and Emma squeezed past her and left the room.

Rikki waited until the door had closed behind them, lent on it and let out a loud sigh of relief.

"*That* was weird!" she said, blowing her hair

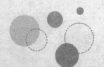
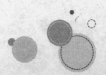

off her forehead as she gave Cleo a sceptical sidelong glance.

Cleo knew what Rikki was getting at, but she didn't want to be mean about Elliot behind Emma's back. Emma was her best friend in the world and Cleo knew how much she loved her little brother. She shrugged her shoulders at Rikki in response. Although Cleo had to admit to herself, she was *much* happier just watching it all unfold than she would have been if she'd been the one getting cards and chocolates from an eleven-year-old boy.

*It's actually kind of sweet when you think about it!* Cleo thought to herself. *Just so long as he doesn't decide he has a crush on me next!*

"Want to practise some more with our powers?" asked Cleo, hastily changing the subject. She nodded over to Emma's sodden, crumpled homework and raised her eyebrows in challenge.

"Yeah, right," Rikki said with a mischievous

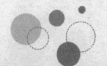
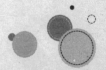

smile, "and invoke the full force of Emma's wrath? We'd be safer putting water balloons in her pillows than we'd be messing about any more with her homework."

"Let's just try on her clothes then," Cleo said decisively, pulling on one of Emma's old swimming caps as she said so and modelling it in front of the mirror. At least that got a laugh out of Rikki and lightened the mood in the room a bit.

Once they were downstairs and far enough away from her room that there was no chance Cleo and Rikki could hear them, Emma gently put her arm around Elliot's shoulders and sat him down on the couch in the lounge-room.

Emma had always known this day would have to come, but she'd been dreading it! Of course it was inevitable that Elliot would be interested in girls one day, but did it have to be now and with a girl five years older than

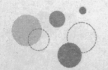
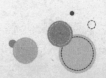

him, a friend of hers and a mermaid to boot! It seemed to Emma that this was like three different relationship problems rolled into one big complicated impossible one!

*Where do I start?* she thought anxiously to herself as she looked into Elliot's open, honest face as he waited expectantly for her to say what was on her mind.

"Elliot, what's going on between you and Rikki?" she asked as considerately as she could. Emma had watched the way he'd been acting around Rikki ever since she'd arrived that evening and it didn't take an Einstein to work out that Elliot had a *huge* crush on Rikki. Emma knew she'd have to handle the situation with tact. She didn't want to see her little brother get hurt, but at the same time, the idea of Elliot having a crush on one of her friends was just ridiculous. Emma knew she had to put an end to it before it got out of hand and the sooner the better for everyone concerned!

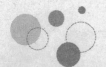

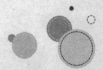

"Don't worry," Elliot told her sincerely, putting a consoling hand on her arm. "I promise our love won't get in the way of your friendship."

*Oh brother, he* has *got it bad!* said Emma to herself, trying to keep a straight face.

"Elliot," she said, placing her hand over his to make him realize that what she was about to say next was important and he should pay attention. "Rikki's not like the girls you go to school with. She's not the kind of girl for you. She's older, and more mature. Kind of," she added, thinking for a second about how many immature things Rikki had done and said since they'd met.

"Some of us men like that in a woman," said Elliot simply.

*Men! Right*, thought Emma. *This isn't going to be easy.*

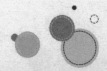

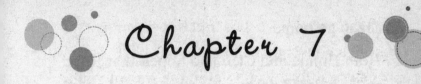

# Chapter 7

The next morning at the Juice-Net Café, Emma and Cleo sat at their usual table, neither knowing where to look. Rikki sat opposite them, glaring as Elliot pulled up a chair and squeezed himself into position to the right of her. It was obvious that Emma's little chat with Elliot hadn't made any difference. He was just as keen as he'd ever been!

The previous evening, when Emma had gone back upstairs to her room after talking to him in the lounge, Elliot had just followed her up, walked straight into her room and sat down next to Rikki. He'd not said anything; he'd just gazed up at her while she tried to read one of Emma's magazines. Emma had suggested a couple of times that he go downstairs to play his skate game, but even that hadn't worked and eventually, Rikki had just decided it was

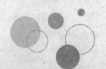

easier to go home.

Both Emma and Cleo had hoped that Rikki might've calmed down a bit after a good night's sleep, but they could see by the tense way she held her shoulders that Rikki was anything but calm. Every time Elliot even so much as breathed, Cleo saw the corners of Rikki's mouth tighten with annoyance. *No, annoyance doesn't really cover how Rikki is feeling at all*, thought Cleo idly. *This is much more like... rage.*

"Is there something you wanted to say to me?" Rikki asked them coldly as Elliot continued to edge his chair closer to hers until he was practically sitting in her lap.

"Well, no," Emma answered cautiously. She didn't want to give Rikki any reason to snap, which was exactly what she expected was going to happen if they didn't handle the situation as carefully as possible. *She's a ticking time bomb!* thought Emma reluctantly.

"When *exactly* did we become babysitters again?" Rikki asked irritably, gesturing towards Elliot, just in case there was any possible confusion as to exactly what was bugging her.

"Elliot, can you just…" Emma started to say, thinking that perhaps if she had *another* older-sister–younger-brother type chat, he might get the message this time. Although she had to admit to herself, it seemed doubtful he'd listen. When Elliot had heard her on the phone that morning, making plans to meet the girls down at the Juice-Net, he'd excitedly asked her what time they were meeting and if he could come with her.

"You *never* take me anywhere!" he'd whined.

"That's not true," she'd calmly replied. "I took you to the greenhouse and your surfing lesson only yesterday."

"Yeah, but you left me to go off with Byron though didn't you?" Elliot had said accusingly.

"Okay, you can come," she'd said ungraciously. But Elliot hadn't even heard the tone in her voice; he was already halfway to his room to collect his jacket.

And now here he was, fawning all over Rikki and ruining the whole morning!

But just as she was about to decoy Elliot away for another heart-to-heart, Wilfred, the manager of the Juice-Net, arrived with their drinks order.

"Two herb juices, one mango smoothie and a banana sundae," said Wilfred cheerfully as he gave the girls their drinks before finally placing the sundae in front of Elliot. It was obvious he hadn't even noticed the tension at the table as he clapped Elliot kindly on the back and asked, "So, did your girlfriend like the chocolates?"

Rikki's heart sank. She didn't think she'd be able to stomach her smoothie after all.

"He's a right gentleman *this* one," Wilfred continued, giving Elliot a friendly nudge on the

arm, "came in with his piggy bank and spent every cent he had. She must be *quite* a girl!"

Rikki literally sunk deeper into her chair with every word.

*Perhaps I could just slip right under the table where no one can see me!* She just hoped no one at the other tables was close enough to hear what was going on. It was bad enough that Cleo and Emma knew!

"She sure is!" Elliot told Wilfred proudly, huddling up even closer to Rikki.

And that was about all Rikki could stand!

"We need to talk," she said to Cleo and Emma, rapidly bounding to her feet as soon as Wilfred was out of earshot. "Stay!" she barked at Elliot as he made to get up and follow them.

Elliot's face crumpled in shock.

"Wait right here," Cleo told him gently, patting his hand as she scrambled out of the booth to follow Emma and Rikki over to the

other side of the café.

Thankfully, a couple of boys they vaguely knew from school had just finished their game of pool as the girls made their way over to that corner of the café. It was as far away as they could get from where Elliot sat, short of going outside, and Emma and Cleo could see that he was happily digging into his sundae and wouldn't hear a word of what they said.

"It's *so* sweet!" Cleo blurted out tactlessly when she caught up with Emma and Rikki, who were already standing behind the pool table. "He has a crush on you."

"HA! Yeah, sweet like a *lemon*," Rikki snapped back, picking up one of the pool cues and bouncing it restlessly from one hand to the other as she spoke. "Did *you* know about this?" she asked Emma accusingly.

"Well, not *exactly*," stammered Emma. "Rikki, don't hurt his fe–"

Rikki threw up her hands, palms out, as if to

stop Emma in her tracks.

"Don't even *think* about asking me to humour him," interrupted Rikki, "because it's not going to happen."

"Can you at least be gentle?" Emma asked pleadingly.

"He's a sweet kid," Cleo added. "There's no need to totally humiliate him or anything."

"You're all *disturbed*," Rikki almost barked back at them both, slamming the pool cue back in its rack in frustration.

*Why can't they see this from my point of view for a change, instead of it being all about Elliot?* she thought irately. *Would either of* them *like a kid chasing after them like this? I'd love to see just how sweet* they'd *be if they were in my shoes.*

"Why is everything sweet and nice with you two all the time?" Rikki asked bitterly.

"Rikki, it's his first crush," Emma said

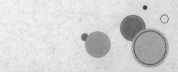

persuasively. "Don't you remember what it was like to be a kid?"

"No, I don't," Rikki answered without hesitation. "And besides," she added. "This is all just because I saved his life."

Not that Rikki regretted saving Elliot's life at all; of course she didn't. But really, the price she was paying for it was ridiculously high! And Cleo and Emma were refusing to see that Elliot was going to suffer no matter how gently Rikki handled it.

"It's like pulling a thorn out of a dog's foot," she told them, hoping a logical argument like this would at least convince Emma to see things from her point of view. Rikki wasn't so sure that Cleo would get the comparison.

"Well, you'd do that gently, wouldn't you?" Emma suggested, not understanding where Rikki was coming from at all.

"Duh, no, I'd do it fast and hope I didn't get bitten," Rikki replied; disappointed Emma

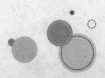

didn't see what she was getting at.

*This isn't working at all*, thought Rikki. *I've got to find some other way to persuade them to see things differently. It's like they expect me to just play along with this whole crush thing no matter what I feel about it or how it might affect Elliot in the long run; but they're obviously not convinced by the tough love argument.*

"Okay, you know what?" she said more calmly. "I don't do the whole 'relationship' thing very well."

"It's not a *relationship*," Cleo said, looking utterly disgusted by the idea. "He's *eleven*."

Rikki inhaled and exhaled deeply in an effort to keep her temper in check.

"*Okay*," Rikki explained as if to a five-year-old. "I don't do the whole people-liking-me thing very well." *There*, she thought to herself, *I can't put it any plainer than that.*

It wasn't as if Rikki had chosen to feel that way or even enjoyed being like that; it

was just the way it *was*. She simply didn't feel comfortable when people liked her, in *that* way at least. It wasn't as if she had trouble with friends liking her, but when boys liked her in the *liked her* kind of way, all she wanted to do was run. Rikki hoped that Emma and Cleo would understand because she didn't want to have to go into her history in that area…

"What's the solution then?" Emma asked, not getting it at all.

"Oh, forget it!" Rikki snapped, realizing it was a waste of time. She didn't know how she could explain it any better than she had.

*How can I get someone to understand a feeling they've obviously never experienced before?* she thought helplessly.

And even *if* Rikki could've found a way to explain her emotions any better, at that point, she couldn't be bothered. Rikki knew when she'd been beaten and this was one of those times.

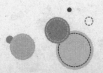

Rikki sighed again and rubbed her eyes furiously.

"Tell me what to say to get him off my case, and I'll say it," she said flatly, all hint of animation gone. *There*, she thought to herself, *if that's what they want, then they've got it.*

But where Rikki had expected Emma and Cleo to burst immediately into lengthy word-for-word descriptions of exactly what they wanted her to say to Elliot, there was instead only silence, the three girls looking at each other blankly.

"I've got nothing," Cleo said finally, breaking the awkward quiet.

"Me neither," Emma added sheepishly.

It looked like they'd have to get some advice on how to let a boy down gently. And without saying another word, all three of them knew *exactly* where to get it.

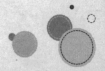

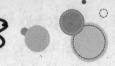

# Chapter 8

The girls had taken a short detour to Emma's house to drop Elliot off on their way to the greenhouse. Elliot couldn't understand why he was being left behind, but he knew he didn't have any choice in the matter. Emma *had* taken him to the Juice-Net *and* bought him an ice-cream sundae; he couldn't expect the world!

Lewis was hard at work in Lenny's office when the three girls finally arrived at the greenhouse. They were lucky Lewis was in there and not somewhere in the depths of the greenhouse proper; there was no need to spend hours trying to find him in that maze of plants! As they walked through the door, they saw Lewis with a soldering iron in one hand and some wire cutters in the other. His face was covered in sweat and he looked like he'd been working hard the whole morning – it appeared

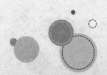

that things with the automated sprinkler system weren't going quite as smoothly as planned.

Even so, when they told him all about Elliot's crush on Rikki, he listened intently to every word they said, taking in the full complexity of the problem even while he kept working. The look on his face as the story unfolded suggested to the girls that he was slightly bemused by it all and he barely held back a laugh when Rikki told him about the chocolates! But a particularly prickly look from Cleo and an even more pointed glare from Rikki told him that now was definitely not the time to be laughing.

"So, what do you suggest I do?" asked Rikki at the end of the recitation.

"And you're asking me *because*...?" Lewis asked, a little confused about why they'd come to him in the first place.

"Well, we figured you would've been rejected a few times," said Rikki matter-of-

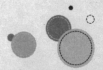

factly. "Surely you'd know a few methods that work."

"Ha!" Lewis laughed, not nearly as offended as he probably ought to have been!

He was just putting the finishing touches on the sprinkler system's control panel and was concentrating on the calibration of a large timing dial that would regulate the entire system. He'd divided the dial into three equal parts, each one designed to trigger the watering of each of the three sections he'd divided the greenhouse into. If it all worked as he'd planned it, the whole automated system would run like clockwork. Lenny would never have to think about watering his plants again!

"Lewis?" snapped Emma, trying in vain to get his attention.

"Hmmm?" replied Lewis absently. "Yes, hold on a minute."

From outside they heard the crunch of gravel as someone approached the office.

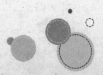

"I need this up and running soon Lewis!" they heard Lenny call through the open window.

"Yeah, I'm almost there!" Lewis yelled back too loudly, as Lenny had already walked into the office by then and was standing in the doorway right next to him.

"Er, right," said Lewis, finally looking up to see Lenny standing there beside him and lowering his voice accordingly. "Every day at five o'clock," he continued, "each of the three sections will be watered in one minute intervals."

"That's a bit short isn't it?" Lenny asked, looking rather concerned.

"Nah, it'll allow for absorption," Lewis reassured him, clearly proud of his work. "So you won't be wasting water. And the cycle will repeat twenty times."

"Ahhh, that sounds better," Lenny said happily, as he headed back out of the office;

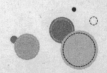

"can't have my plants going thirsty."

"No chance of that," Lewis called after him.

"*Lewis*?" Emma interrupted once more. "Boy advice, *please*?"

"Ah, yeah," Lewis started and then ran out of steam. He had to admit, he felt a little uncomfortable being asked about the ways girls had successfully dumped him, although he couldn't quite put his finger on why. He looked up at them all for a moment – the fact that Cleo was there that was making him very uncomfortable. *That's weird*, he thought to himself. *I've always been able to say pretty much whatever's on my mind around her.*

Realizing that his silence was starting to become awkward, Lewis decided to be direct and to the point.

"Most guys just wanna know where they stand…" he began.

"Told you," Rikki interrupted, glaring at Emma.

"... without having to feel like a loser," Lewis finished.

"Told you," Emma smiled back at Rikki.

"Will the crush wear off on its own?" Cleo asked, ignoring her friends' good natured bickering.

"Not in my experience," Lewis half-mumbled, hoping that Cleo wouldn't catch the unexpected gloominess in his voice.

"Hey, Lewis!" Lenny shouted through the window, breaking the awkward silence. "Time *is* money."

Emma held up her hands as if to silence Lenny and smiled half-apologetically at Lewis.

"It's okay," Emma said as she walked towards the door. "We were just leaving."

Rikki and Cleo waved their goodbyes and followed her out quickly, leaving Lewis to gaze after Cleo for a second or two before shaking his head in an effort to lighten his mood.

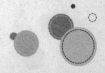

*Brave little kid* he said to himself, thinking of Elliot. *He's got guts, that's for sure.*

Rikki walked along the beach and thought about how, on days as perfect as this one, she'd ordinarily be on the phone to Cleo and Emma trying to persuade them to meet her at their secret cove for a swim.

But the whole Elliot thing had come between them! Now when Rikki saw her friends, she half-expected them to launch into a lecture about the dos and don'ts of breaking a kid's heart! And she knew they felt equally ill at ease around her…

What made it really tough, though, was that the three of them had already been through the whole thing and hadn't come up with any solutions. What was the point going over and over old ground?

Given the choice, Rikki would've always chosen to be swimming *in* the water rather than

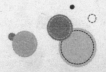

just walking alongside it, but the way things had unfolded over the last few days, the idea of swimming alone just felt wrong. She knew that instead of the thrill she'd usually get as she powered through the water, all she'd be thinking of was how much she wished that Cleo and Emma were there with her.

And when Rikki really thought about it, if she had to name the thing she loved most about being a mermaid, that was it – swimming with Cleo and Emma. Not the powers, not the fact that being a mermaid made her unique, just the swimming with her friends.

And that was what annoyed her most about the whole Elliot situation – that all three of them had allowed it to come between them.

Still, even though Rikki knew that it was hurting their friendship, she couldn't see things Cleo and Emma's way just to get things back to normal!

Of course she'd try to be gentle with Elliot, but what if he just wouldn't listen? What if he

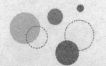
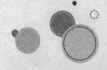

always had this crush on her? Was she going
to have to pretend it didn't bother her just to
keep her friends happy forever? To pretend
to be okay with something just because your
friends wanted you to just seemed a bit shallow
somehow. *Well, not just a bit shallow*, Rikki
thought, *a lot shallow*.

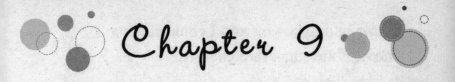

# Chapter 9

"Hey Rikki," Elliot shouted, running along the beach to catch up with her.

"Oh, Elliot, what a surprise," she muttered, quickening her pace a bit.

"I bought you something," said Elliot excitedly, doing an odd half-run half-skip in an effort to keep up with her.

"Look, Elliot, no more presents, alright?" Rikki said tiredly.

Elliot looked dejected for a second. "Okay," he said gloomily.

Rikki saw that he was clutching something – it looked like a small glass figurine – behind his back, but whatever it was she didn't want it. All Rikki wanted was for him to leave her alone.

But it'd take more than that to permanently dampen Elliot's enthusiasm! "Hey, I was

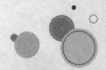

thinking maybe you and I could catch a movie?" he suggested eagerly.

"No thanks," Rikki answered flatly, increasing her pace.

"Well, we could see anything you like," Elliot offered as he suddenly grabbed hold of Rikki's hand.

And *that* was about as much as Rikki could stand. Chocolates and cards and having to listen to him go on and on about how absolutely incredible he thought she was, was one thing, but putting up with him actually trying to hold her hand on the beach!? That was too much. Rikki felt the blood pumping in her head; she knew she was losing her temper. And right then, she didn't care how much everyone wanted her to protect Elliot's feelings.

"Hey!" she snapped, stopping dead on the spot and jerking her hand sharply from his grasp. "I know you've got a crush on me, but *I'm not interested*!"

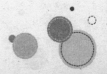

"Did you know I'm gonna be a professional surfer?" Elliot went on, completely undeterred.

*It's like he can't hear me!* thought Rikki helplessly.

"Elliot," Rikki said in a measured tone, trying as hard as she could to remain calm, "the fact is, I'm not a girlfriend kind of girl. I'm a loner. That's how I like it." *There*, she thought, *that's about as gentle and caring as I can be. But if he keeps this up, he's going to see my not-so-gentle side.*

"What if I became a loner too?" Elliot suggested keenly. "Then we could both be loners, together."

The hope in Elliot's eyes as he said it was almost heartbreaking. The poor kid really did have quite a massive crush on her, but all Rikki wanted to do was get rid of him. *This isn't my problem!* she thought. *The kid's got to grow up one day and he's going to be hurt whether he likes it or not. It's not that I want to be the first*

*one to break his heart, but he chose me for the
job and there's nothing I can do about it!*

She'd finally reached the point where being
gentle and tactful didn't matter any more. All
Rikki wanted, more than anything else, was
for this whole Elliot situation to stop being her
problem. She'd had enough.

"Look," she said, turning to Elliot and
looking him straight in the eye. Her voice was
like crackling ice and her eyes just as cold.
"Even if you were four years older, two feet
taller and a whole lot less... squeaky clean, I
would *not* be interested. In the real world, no
means no, so *BACK OFF*!!!"

Rikki had seen the look of hurt on Elliot's
face as soon as she'd started to speak, but once
she started, she just wasn't able to stop. And
in a way, Rikki didn't *want* to stop. *The kid
needs to know*, she thought resignedly. By the
time she'd finished saying what she'd needed

to, she could see that Elliot was close to tears, but as bad as she knew she'd feel about it later, Rikki's sympathy levels had run completely dry by then. All she wanted was for the whole 'Elliot thing' to be over.

Rikki finished speaking and stormed off up the beach, leaving Elliot where he stood. Thankfully for Elliot, she didn't turn back, or she would have seen the tears begin to stream down his face.

When she reached the top of the sand dunes, Rikki looked back to see if Elliot was still where she'd left him. Even though she was a long way away, she could tell by the way his shoulders were hunched over that he was taking it really badly. As Rikki watched, Elliot reached into his pocket and pulled something out. He looked at it for a minute and then with all of his strength, he threw whatever it was out into the water, where it splashed into the sea just beyond the breakers.

Rikki pulled her jacket around herself tightly against the wind. As horrible as it was to see Elliot in that state, and knowing that she was the cause of it all, Rikki felt there was absolutely nothing more she could do. If she went back now to console him, he'd be filled with false hope and that would be even crueller.

Reluctantly, she turned and continued on her way, leaving Elliot staring out to sea.

*He'll get over it,* she thought optimistically, *he's a tough little kid and this is only going to make him tougher.*

The next day, Rikki finally found some time to herself with no one around telling her what to do or how to act. No Elliot telling her how much he loved her and no Emma and Cleo telling her how she should let him down gently. She'd found a booth to herself at the Juice-Net Café and had sat there all morning, staring vacantly into her smoothie and thinking about

absolutely nothing. Every minute of it had been complete, stress-free bliss.

When Emma and Cleo walked through the door, Rikki was happier to see them than she'd been in ages.

"Hey guys, what's up?" she asked as soon as they got to her table. But from the looks on their faces she could tell things weren't going to stay stress-free for long. Cleo and Emma didn't seem happy to see *her* at all.

"We can't find Elliot," Cleo said sharply.

"He'll be around," Rikki said vaguely, trying to stay upbeat. "Just relax."

"He's not, Rikki," Emma said irritably, clearly she was in no mood to relax. "We've looked all over and he's not anywhere. It's not like him to just disappear."

"Have you told your parents?" Rikki asked hopefully.

"No way," Emma answered. "They'd freak

out. It's like he's run away. You know, he was acting all weird last night. Not his usual happy self."

Rikki felt the now familiar churning in the pit of her stomach. She knew precisely why Elliot wouldn't have been his normal happy self. And as much as she'd tried to put the events of yesterday out of her mind, Rikki was aware of an underlying feeling of guilt. The minute the words had come out of her mouth she regretted saying them, but it wasn't her fault! She was just being honest, and if the kid couldn't handle a bit of honesty, then that was his problem, not hers. Still, something about it just didn't feel right. Perhaps she *could've* been a bit gentler on him. But she'd *tried* so hard; she'd just got to the point where she couldn't try any more. Oh, maybe this *was* her fault after all!

"What?" Emma asked, seeing the tortured look on Rikki's face.

"Oh, nah, it's probably just…" Rikki

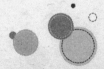

muttered, delaying the inevitable. She knew she'd have to tell them exactly what she'd said to Elliot.

"*Rikki*!" Emma snapped impatiently.

"*Okay*!" Rikki replied. "I told him that I wasn't interested. But I *think* I was gentle."

Both Emma and Cleo raised their eyebrows in disbelief and looked at her to carry on with the story because they all knew there was more to it than Rikki was letting on.

"Okay," Rikki went on, realizing that honesty was the best policy and if the kid *had* disappeared as Cleo and Emma thought, there was no time to lose. "I told him that even if he was older, taller and a lot less... I think the words were... squeaky clean, that I wouldn't be interested and that he should just back off and leave me alone."

Rikki grimaced. Yes, she'd meant to give them the no-holds-barred version of what happened, but now that it was out in the open,

it seemed terribly *harsh*.

Cleo and Emma started talking in unison.

"*Rikki*!" Cleo screeched in shock.

"He's just a *kid*," said Emma, visibly upset.

"He kept *bugging* me," was all Rikki thought to say in her defence, as she stared down at the table to avoid the critical looks she could still feel boring into her skull.

"You keep acting like he's committing a crime for having a crush on you," said Emma furiously as she banged the table with the palm of her hand.

Rikki looked up in shock. She'd never seen Emma act so passionately before.

"We've got to go find him before my parents find out," said Emma urgently. "But if anything happens to him," and here she stopped and looked deeply into Rikki's eyes, "it'll be *your* fault."

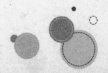

# Chapter 10

The sound of the door banging closed behind Emma and Cleo felt, to Rikki, like a slap in the face.

She couldn't remember feeling so completely and utterly miserable. *How can all this be happening to me*, she thought. *It's not my fault the kid had a crush on me. I didn't ask for it. All I did was fish him out of the water after his sister practically abandoned him and left me to do all her dirty work.* She honestly couldn't imagine how she could have handled things any better than she had. *Well*, she thought sadly, *perhaps I didn't need to tell him he was 'squeaky clean', but aside from that I just said what needed to be said.*

But Rikki knew this was about more than the way she'd spoken to Elliot, this was just another glaring example of the way she conducted all her relationships: *very badly.*

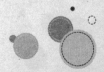

Rikki sat at the table, her head resting in her hands, and stared miserably at the swirling pattern of the tabletop. Her thoughts tumbled so violently around in her head that she didn't even hear Lewis call her name.

"Hey," he repeated, his face reflecting the concern in his voice. "Why the long face?"

"Elliot," Rikki mumbled.

*Ahhh, nothing serious then, just more of the same angst!* Lewis thought to himself, pleased that he wasn't going to have to give out more advice or listen to any new hard-luck stories. *These girls really take it out of a guy!*

"*Oo-ooh*, let me guess," he said with a relieved tone. "You tried to let him down easy, and now he's mortally crushed."

"He's gone missing, Lewis," Rikki said grimly, finally looking up from the table. "This is *serious*. Have you seen him anywhere?" she asked hopefully.

Lewis thought carefully. He remembered seeing Elliot at the greenhouse and as he'd

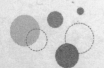

been working on the automated sprinkler system pretty much 24-7 since then; that must've been the *last* time he'd seen him.

"No, no I haven't," Lewis answered. "Not since Lenny's."

Rikki's head dropped back into her hands.

"Hey, don't give up so easily!" Lewis said, sitting down. "One of my *many* brothers collects bugs – he thinks he's a bit of a junior entomologist actually – and he always says that if you want to *catch* a butterfly, you have to *think* like a butterfly."

Rikki looked up slowly.

"This better be going somewhere, Lewis," she said dismally.

"Yeah, of course it is. All I'm saying is maybe you should try thinking like a little kid?" said Lewis.

"Hmmph, easier said than done," Rikki told him. "Where would *you* hide if you were a little kid?"

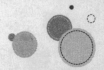

"*Duh*! Somewhere *you'd* never find me," Lewis replied, as if it was the most obvious thing in the world.

Suddenly, something in Rikki's head clicked.

*I've heard that before... or seen something somewh–*

"That's *it*!" Rikki exclaimed as she jumped to her feet, sending her chair crashing backwards onto the floor.

"*What*?" Lewis called.

But Rikki was already racing out of the door.

"I've no time to explain," Rikki yelled over her shoulder. "But thank *yooooou*."

And before Lewis could say another word to her, Rikki was gone.

"Alright," Lewis said to the now-empty table, "be mysterious."

Rikki *had* suddenly remembered something and although there was no way he could've known it, Lewis had given her the perfect clue to where Elliot could be found. It was something

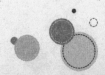

Elliot had said when they'd first gone to Lenny's greenhouse that Saturday morning, something about being able to hide in there *forever*...

Rikki sprinted along the canal bank, around past Cleo's house and the marina, right to the greenhouse without stopping, her heart thumping so loudly in her chest she thought she'd faint.

She didn't have the slightest doubt that Elliot was where she thought he'd be – hidden somewhere amongst the tangle of plants. *He has to be there...* she thought frantically.

"Elliot!" Rikki shouted, before she was even properly through the greenhouse gate. "*Elliot*! I know you're in here. *Please* come out."

Rikki stopped and listened for the crunch of gravel or any other sign that Elliot might be nearby, but she could hardly hear a thing over the sound of her own breathy wheeze. She gulped down some air and shouted Elliot's name again.

Rikki didn't know what she was going to

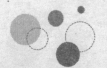

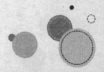

say to Elliot when she finally found him. All she knew was that she had to make things right again. Not only right with Elliot, but right with Emma and Cleo as well.

She was sick of the hostile feeling she'd encountered every time she'd met up with them lately. And Rikki knew she wasn't entirely blameless either.

What she wanted more than *anything* was for things to be back the way they were before. *If only my power was to be able to turn back time!* Rikki thought sadly.

And whether Rikki liked it or not – and she had to admit she *didn't* – she knew for sure that the only way to mend her strained relationship with Emma and Cleo was to find Elliot and make it up to him somehow. It was the somehow that was the problem.

*I'll just have to make it up as I go along,* thought Rikki determinedly.

It seemed to Rikki as if the path wound around in circles, there were so few landmarks,

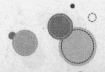

but after getting lost for the third or fourth time, she recognized something familiar.

*I think I was standing here when Emma told me about the surfing lessons… oh, and here's that weird rock I kicked… the clearing has to be around here somewhere.*

"Elliot," Rikki called, knowing she was close. "*Elliot?*"

She parted the thick ferns and looked down around the small clearing.

Elliot sat on the ground in a tight ball, his knees drawn up under his chin, his arms hugging his legs. He didn't look up.

"Sorry," Rikki said as she pushed a few more branches out of the way and entered the clearing. "It's nearly closing time," she added jokingly.

Elliot didn't respond.

"I remembered you said you could hide in here forever," she added, kneeling down beside him. "Elliot, are you okay?" she asked softly.

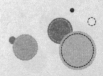

"I'm *fine*," he answered, his voice full of tears. "*Just leave me alone*."

"Listen, Elliot," Rikki began, choosing her words with care. "I'm sorry about all that stuff I said yesterday, it's just that... ever since I was little... I'm used to people not liking me."

She stopped suddenly and thought about what she was going to say next. Rikki didn't want to spill her entire life story to an eleven-year old, but Elliot did deserve to know the real reason behind why she'd acted the way she had. It would've been a lot easier to just tell him she already had a boyfriend or something like that, but that didn't seem very fair at all. She only hoped he was old enough to understand...

"I'm used to people not liking me," Rikki repeated. "But when people *like* me, it's not so easy. It makes me feel like... I don't even think I can explain it... it makes me feel like I'm fenced in or something and I don't handle it very well."

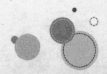

Rikki shrugged her shoulders. There was so much more to say, but already she felt frustrated with her own inability to put her muddled thoughts into words.

"I'm *sorry* Elliot," Rikki finished lamely. "Reckon you could try to understand?"

Elliot heard the note of defeat in her voice and looked up.

"Can we still hang out together sometimes?" he asked in a small voice.

Rikki smiled.

"If we're ever going to hang out together," she said as she got up and hauled Elliot to his feet, "we've gotta get out of here first!"

Rikki gave him a friendly shove out through the plants and Elliot laughed. For the first time in what seemed like a long while, Rikki thought that things might just turn out okay.

# Chapter 11

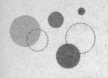
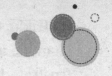

Lenny looked at his watch. *Almost five o'clock already!* he thought happily as he locked his tools up in the office and took out his MP3 player. *Time for me to see if Lewis's handiwork is all it's cracked up to be!*

He strolled over to the main gate of the greenhouse, took out one of his earphones and listened for a moment. He heard a loud *CLICK*! as the automatic locking device slotted loudly into place. *Whaddya know, it works!* Lenny smiled to himself; he knew Lewis could do it!

He rattled the gate just to be sure and seeing it was all secure, Lenny stuck his earphone back in, cranked up his MP3 player and strolled off down the path, humming tunelessly to himself.

But as pleased as Lenny was about it, the success of the automated lock spelled disaster

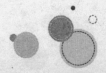

for Rikki and Elliot! For the moment though, the locked gate was the least of their worries.

"I think the entrance is *this* way," said Rikki as they ducked under some low-lying branches and weaved their way through the thick foliage.

But it wasn't just the winding paths that led nowhere and the thought of Emma still out there somewhere, afraid for her brother's safety, that were troubling Rikki.

She stared up at the network of pipes that hung threateningly above their heads.

*It was around four or four-fifteen when I left the Juice-Net Café. I guess it took... about twenty minutes to get here... say another twenty minutes to find Elliot...*

It was close to five and Rikki knew it!

All that she could hope for now was that they still had some time up their sleeves and that Lewis's expertise with the automated sprinkler system wasn't as great as he seemed to think it was.

*All right, this is getting dangerous.* Rikki thought, trying to keep calm. *If those sprinklers come on, there's no question that I'll be flapping my tail in the dirt before I know what's hit me. And if Elliot sees that, we're in serious trouble.*

Rikki put her hand on Elliot's shoulder and steered him down yet another path, peering from side to side without seeing anything that even remotely resembled the way out.

Rikki felt her skin begin to prickle with fear. The three of them had gone to a lot of effort to convince Elliot and Cleo's sister, Kim, that there had been no truth to the mermaid diary they'd found a couple of weeks back. But if Elliot saw her transform into a so-called mythical figure now... *oh it just doesn't bear thinking about!*

Rikki needed help and she needed it fast!

*Think, think... don't get hysterical. Lewis! I need to call Lewis! Perhaps he can deactivate the sprinkler system remotely*, she thought, fighting down her rising panic. *That'd be precisely the*

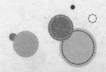

*kind of extra feature he'd think of building into a system like this.*

Rikki took a deep breath, scrambled around in her bag for her mobile phone and selected Lewis's number from her contacts.

The phone rang and rang. Rikki felt the sweat begin to bead on her forehead.

*C'mon, c'mon, answer, will you?*

Lewis stood on the jetty, fishing rod and bait already loaded securely onto his boat. After being cooped up in a greenhouse for practically the whole weekend, Lewis knew a couple of hours' fishing was exactly what he needed to unwind. *A bit of stress-free relaxation will fix me right up!* he thought cheerfully.

Lewis looked doubtfully at the telephone number displayed on his mobile and exhaled loudly. *Gah! This better be good, Rikki!* he thought irritably.

"*Hello?*" he answered casually.

"Lewis, what time do the sprinklers come

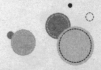

105

on?" he heard Rikki's voice ask him from down the phone.

"The watering system starts at five," Lewis replied, sounding bored, *"why?"*

Rikki turned her back and held the phone close to her mouth so Elliot wouldn't hear her.

"Listen, Lewis," Rikki explained. "We're in the greenhouse and we're lost."

*"What?"* asked Lewis. Rikki was talking so quietly, so as not to frighten Elliot, that Lewis could barely hear her.

"Lewis! Listen to me," Rikki whispered harshly. "I went looking for Elliot and found him in the greenhouse. He was right in the middle somewhere and now I don't think we're going to be able to find our way out before the sprinklers start up."

*"You what?"* screeched Lewis, only now beginning to understand the seriousness of the situation Rikki and Elliot were in.

"Lewis!" Rikki almost yelled in frustration.

"We *need* your help! If we don't get out of here before the sprinklers start, you know *exactly* what kind of a disaster zone this is going to turn into. Get down here now! And if you can find them, get Emma and Cleo here too."

"Oh, okay," Lewis stammered, finally comprehending the enormity of what Rikki was saying.

"I'm um, I'm on my way," he spluttered, hanging up the phone and texting Emma and Cleo with one hand while he grabbed his fishing rod with the other and bolted up the jetty towards Lenny's place.

"Elliot, quick, *run*!" Rikki yelled when she'd hung up the phone, grabbing Elliot's arm and dragging him down the first path she saw.

"Why are we running?" Elliot asked, panting alongside of her. Thankfully he could ask questions and run at the same time! Behind them, Rikki heard the first section of sprinklers

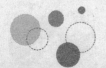

suddenly burst into life, raining water down on the plants they'd just run past.

Frantically, they raced through the nursery, darting left and right whenever they saw an open path, sometimes racing back in the direction they'd come from whenever they struck a dead end. Rikki still had no idea which way led to the front gate, but at least now she knew the general direction they had to run in – *away from the sprinklers*. And if that way led them closer to the gate, then great, but if not, then there was really nothing she could do about it! All Rikki knew for sure was that they *had* to keep running away from whichever direction they heard water.

"This way," Rikki shouted to Elliot as the second section of sprinklers started up behind them.

"Right," said Rikki, suddenly stopping to get her bearings when she felt they were safe from the sprinklers for a minute or two.

"So *this* is section two." If they could just

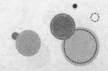

keep ahead of whichever section of sprinklers was next scheduled to start up, they'd be fine. But they could only keep running for so long before the sprinklers eventually caught up with them.... *I hope Lewis is on his way*, she thought. *With Emma and Cleo not far behind!*

Elliot stood beside her gulping down air and trying to get his breath back.

"What's wrong?" he panted. "Why are we running?"

But Rikki was too busy to listen – her mind raced as she searched her memory for *anything* Lewis might've said about the watering system that might help them now.

"What did Lewis say?" Rikki asked aloud, more to herself than Elliot. "What was the interval between watering every section?"

"You're asking *me*?" Elliot replied, staring up at her blankly. "I dunno." He shrugged his shoulders uncomprehendingly.

"I think it was a minute," mumbled Rikki,

trying to remember back to their conversation in Lenny's office.

She came to herself and looked down at Elliot's confused expression.

"Sorry, Elliot," she said, before hearing a sprinkler very near them start up. "*Run!*"

They ran frantically through the plants, the branches whipping against their faces and legs and almost tripping them up every now and then, sending them stumbling for a pace or two before they regained their balance. But Rikki knew they didn't have time to worry about the odd stumble. They *had* to keep going.

"I think it's this way," Rikki shouted as she veered off to her left. It really didn't matter whether they turned left or right or just kept running straight ahead, just as long as they kept in front of the sprinklers.

Rikki knew she couldn't keep up the pace for much longer. She stopped again, bent over double and gasped for air. Elliot dropped to his knees, breathing heavily.

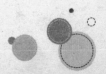

"I don't *get* it," Elliot panted beside her. "What's the big deal? Is something chasing us?"

Rikki really did feel sorry for him now. First he'd had his heart broken and now he was about to have his lungs taken almost to breaking point as well. They had to find the gate and they didn't have much time left. *Surely we can't be far from the entrance now,* she thought. *Even if we started right at the back of the greenhouse, we must have run the entire length of it by now. There can't be that far to go.* The thought spurred her on.

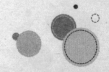

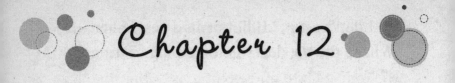

# Chapter 12

Rikki and Elliot turned two more corners and suddenly the gate appeared, looming large before them.

"The gate, Elliot!" Rikki shouted triumphantly. "We've found the gate!"

Elliot didn't think he could work up as much enthusiasm as Rikki could, but he smiled feebly anyway. He felt a bit sick after all the running around they'd just done.

Relieved beyond belief, Rikki slowed down to a walk, put her hands on her hips and breathed deeply to try and catch her breath.

From the other side of the gate, Lewis heard Rikki's cries and he raced over to the heavily barred entrance.

"It's locked," he said miserably when he saw Rikki.

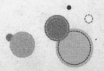

"*No!*" yelled Rikki. And then more quietly, she added, "Don't tell me that I've just broken the four-minute mile getting us out of that maze, only to turn into a mermaid at the entrance... *just don't tell me that, okay*?" she sighed through the bars.

Rikki grabbed hold of the gate with both hands and shook it as hard as she could, grunting with the effort. She knew it was a useless thing to do, but she was just so frustrated.

As if it hadn't been hard enough finding Elliot in the first place, then trying to make things okay with him, then out-running the sprinklers to get where they were now. They were so close and that gate felt like the one thing that could undo all her good work. If she turned into a mermaid now, *everything* would've all been for nothing.

"You can't get out," Lewis said matter-of-factly, pointing at the lock as he spoke. "I installed this yesterday. Automatic lock – *unbreakable.*"

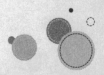

"I guess we're stuck here for a while," Elliot said, looking up at Rikki as if being stuck in there with her wasn't such a bad deal at all.

All of sudden, from behind Lewis they heard running footsteps and Emma and Cleo burst into the greenhouse car park.

"*Elliot!*" cried Emma, rushing at the gate, her voice cracking with relief.

"Yep, I found him," said Rikki, as Emma hugged her little brother tightly through the bars.

"But this might turn ugly," she added, pointing behind her to the rapidly approaching band of water.

The two girls stared up over Rikki's and Elliot's heads and their mouths dropped open in horror.

"Yeah, look, you guys have got about 20 seconds before those sprinklers start," Lewis interrupted, quickly calculating how long it had been since the last section of sprinklers had

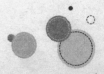

started up.

"So, we get wet," Elliot said, struggling out of Emma's grasp. "What's the big deal?"

Not knowing what else to do, Rikki searched around desperately for something that might help them, a crowbar, some wire cutters, anything. But on her side of the fence, there was nothing. Sure, there was plenty of soil and plants, but they were no help whatsoever. Suddenly though, she spotted a small watering can sitting against the fence on the other side of the gate.

"Cleo!" she whispered frantically, "Cleo!" Catching Cleo's gaze, she glanced quickly down towards the watering can and then up again with a suggestive look. It was their one chance. If Cleo and Emma could somehow use their powers to break the lock, they'd be free. It was a long shot, and they'd have to do it without letting Elliot see anything, but it felt like a chance worth taking.

Rikki turned around to where Elliot was

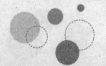

standing. He was already looking back the way they'd come, so he probably wouldn't have noticed what Emma and Cleo were doing anyway, but Rikki knew that there was no point taking any unnecessary chances.

"Is that a lizard?" she asked him casually, pointing in the direction of the thickest bush she could see.

"Where?" Elliot asked, venturing further into the greenhouse in the direction Rikki had indicated.

That was Cleo's cue to act! She rushed over, picked up the watering can and poured it all over the lock, thoroughly saturating it.

"Em!" she shouted, once the lock was ready.

Emma concentrated intently on the lock, feeling out the water that had penetrated deep within the mechanism. She gently gestured with her hand and molecule by molecule, she froze it solid. Slowly at first, and then more rapidly, she felt the water expand as it froze, gradually

forcing the lock apart from within, until with a deafening *CRUNCH!* the entire lock cracked open.

"Elliot!" Rikki shouted as soon as she heard the lock crack open. She raced over to where he was standing, still peering into the plants trying to see the fictional lizard, grabbed his hand and pulled him towards the gate. She kicked it open and darted through, yanking Elliot behind her to the safety of the other side *just* as the first drops of water began to tumble down from the final section of sprinklers.

Emma ran straight to Elliot and threw her arms tightly around him. He tried to wriggle out of her clutches, but she held him fast to her, only letting him go to check to see if he had any bumps or bruises.

"Stop fussing, Emma," said Elliot, embarrassed by the attention. He couldn't understand why everyone was so upset! *So I disappeared for an afternoon, big deal!* he thought crossly, *if this is the reaction I'm going*

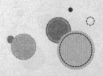

*to get, I'm never going to do* that *again!*

Emma stood up and looked at Rikki. She didn't know how to begin to thank her, so instead she flung her arms around her neck. Emma felt her stiffen, she knew that Rikki wasn't very good with emotions and affection, but there was no way she could possibly vocalize her thanks! *This'll have to do and she'll have to like it!*

Cleo soon joined them, giving both Emma and Rikki a knowing smile.

The relieved look on their faces told the story… relief that Elliot had been found, relief that Rikki had, against all odds, stayed dry and relief that their friendship had survived!

Lewis stood by the gate and stared at the now shattered lock, shaking his head in dismay.

"I told Lenny that lock was going to be unbreakable," he said ruefully. "He'll sue me!"

"Your lock?" Cleo asked him, her eyebrows raised accusingly. "*You* locked them in?"

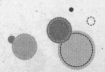

she asked, as if the fact that it was his lock somehow made him responsible for the whole horrible situation.

"It's not *my* fault," Lewis said defensively. "At closing time it locks! It's..." he was about to launch into a full explanation of the benefits of having the gate lock automatically and the various features of that particular lock, but seeing the chastising look on Cleo's face, he suddenly thought better of it. "It's prone to breakage and I'll have to rectify that," he finished, earning himself a warm smile of appreciation from Cleo.

"You guys are weird," Elliot said, looking at them all as if they were half crazy. "Were you running from the *water*?" he asked Rikki.

"Yeah, it's uh... it's my water-based mascara," Rikki replied as nonchalantly as she could, as if worrying about her mascara was the kind of thing she did every day. "It runs everywhere when it's wet."

"Girls are weird," Elliot said with certainty

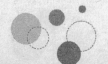
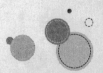

as he, Emma, Rikki and Cleo turned away from the greenhouse gate and started to walk home.

"Elliot, don't *ever* run away again," Emma said, wrapping her arm around Elliot's shoulder and kissing the top of his head in a sisterly kind of way.

"All right," Elliot agreed, wriggling out from under Emma's arm at the same time.

"And, don't tell Mum and Dad," Emma warned him half-jokingly.

"No way," Elliot said, as if that was the last thing he was about to do.

"And don't get a girlfriend till you're old enough," Emma added finally.

"Okay," Elliot replied, not very convincingly at all.

Emma gave him a cautioning kind of look, as if her last bit of advice had been the one she was most serious about, but Elliot just looked the other way towards Rikki and reached out to grab her hand.

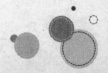

"And don't push your luck," Rikki told him, pulling her hand away from his.

Lewis watched them go; he had some explaining to do when Lenny caught up with him!

Later that afternoon after they'd dropped Elliot home, the three girls made their way down to the beach.

The sun was just beginning to sink below the horizon and there was not a soul around.

*So very different from the last time I was here... with Elliot*, thought Rikki contentedly, *it was a very close call, but it seems that everything has worked out okay.*

"It seems like *ages* since we've been swimming together," Cleo said excitedly.

"It sure does," said Rikki, looking happily over at her two friends. "Race to you the shore break!" she added as she hared off down the beach, with both girls hard on her heels.

They dived into the churning surf and felt the familiar bubbly sensation in their legs before thrashing their tails and propelling themselves out into the sea.

Suddenly something on the ocean floor caught Rikki's eye.

*It's probably just a piece of glass or something,* she thought, diving down to investigate.

The seaweed undulated back and forth, first revealing and then hiding the object. Rikki swam over and dug around in the sand until her fingers felt something.

*What's this?* she thought as she pulled out a small glass dolphin figurine. *Could this be what Elliot threw into the waves?* Rikki thought for a minute; she'd only glimpsed whatever he'd been holding in his hand... but she knew she was right.

*Thank you,* she said softly to herself.

From up ahead, Rikki could hear Emma and

Cleo as they played tag with a pod of chattering dolphins and she smiled to herself.

*Life is pretty much perfect!*